Murder between Brushstrokes

A Little Firling Mystery – Book Four

by Belinda Chavremootoo

Dedication

*For every cat who ever solved a mystery quietly
before the humans caught up.*

Text Copyright

About the Author

Belinda Chavremootoo writes charming cozy mysteries filled with seaside secrets, garden gates, and cats who always know the truth. When she's not plotting fictional crimes, she can be found in her garden, where the scent of soil and the rustle of leaves provide endless inspiration — all under the watchful gaze of her two cats, who supervise with quiet judgment.

Table of Contents

Prologue

The chapel ruins had always been silent.

But that summer, they began to whisper.

Footsteps pressed paths into the grass where no one should have walked. Petals fell from wildflowers without wind. The ivy climbed faster, curling like fingers.

Someone was watching.

Not the painter. Not the student. Not the cat.

Someone else.

Someone who knew the hollow spaces between brushstrokes.

The lies buried under layers of paint.

Someone who had waited long enough.

Chapter 1

The coneflowers were holding court.

Annabel stood by the edge of her garden, tea in hand, watching as the sun caught the backs of the petals — russet, gold, magenta — each one slightly bowed like they knew summer was nearly done performing.

Behind them, the dahlias bloomed like small, regal explosions.

The Heleniums burned bronze and orange like sparks in a fireplace.

Black-eyed Susans nodded in the breeze, and crocosmia shot fiery red flares through a bed that had been mostly green the week before.

They didn't need her now — not really.

A bit of weeding, the odd deadheading, some gentle watering if the rain forgot itself. The tomatoes were nearly ripe, the runner beans overachieving as usual. There was peace in it — the kind that came from knowing something would grow whether or not you hovered over it.

And yet...

She took another sip of tea, lukewarm and vaguely chamomile-adjacent, and tried to ignore the feeling rising up in her chest. Restlessness.

The garden was fine. Beautiful, even.

But she wanted to see what the *wild* things were doing.

***

The knock came like a warning shot: sharp, then immediately followed by a heel-thump against the doorframe.

Annabel sighed. She didn't need to check who it was. No one else knocked like they were trying to evict the door.

She opened it to find Evie Barnes, balancing a thermos, a tote bag, a sketchbook, and something wrapped in wax paper like a crime scene sandwich.

"I made lunch," Evie declared, breezing inside like she lived there. "One of them is either tuna or very bad egg mayo. The other has beetroot and shame. Anyway, we're going. You can't back out now."

Annabel blinked. "Going where?"

"To the art thing. Obviously."

"I said I'd *think* about it."

"You said yes while distracted by aphids. That's binding under village law."

"I don't paint."

"You *notice* things," Evie said, already putting the kettle back on like she didn't trust Annabel's tea. "You think in colour palettes and plant textures. That's painting, just with fewer tantrums and more compost."

Persephone appeared on the windowsill, tail flicking with disapproval. She knocked over a pencil and yawned theatrically.

"I don't have supplies."

Evie tossed her a neatly rolled brush set with all the flair of a magician. "You do now."

***

Foxglove Meadow shimmered in the early afternoon sun.

The grass was tall, golden-tipped, with scattered thistles and delicate yarrow that leaned lazily into the breeze. A few late bees drifted between wildflowers. It smelled of warm grass and nostalgia.

Basil Marlowe had marked the area with coloured bunting and small wooden signs reading *"Observe, don't intrude."*

Evie was unimpressed. "Is that a rule or a threat?"

They were among the first to arrive. Annabel laid out the brush kit and opened her sketchbook, feeling slightly ridiculous and slightly exhilarated. The air smelled different than it did in her garden — looser, wilder. Less hers.

The rest of the group began to arrive.

***

Basil Marlowe, tall and angular with a swept-back silver mane and a scarf that looked like it had lived several dramatic lives, moved among them like a conductor of woodland energy.

"You are not here to replicate, my darlings," he said grandly. "You are here to *witness*. Nature reveals herself only to the reverent observer."

Evie leaned toward Annabel. "Drink every time he says 'reverent' and we'll be plastered by lunch."

***

Claudia Fenwick had already picked a spot by the tall grass. She was dressed in olive green and slate grey, her shirt precisely ironed, her short-cropped hair pinned back like she didn't trust the wind. She unpacked a minimalistic watercolour set with surgical efficiency and didn't greet anyone. Annabel noticed the way Claudia's eyes flicked toward the others — cool, unreadable, waiting.

***

Jules Kepler showed up next, wearing a wide-brimmed straw hat, layered necklaces, and a canvas apron that already had strategically placed paint smudges. He looked like someone who believed in auras and never used the word "beige."

"Vibes are *immaculate*," he announced to no one in particular, setting down his things like he was claiming land. "I can *feel* the energy of the yarrow."

Nell, trailing him, wore a long cardigan that nearly brushed the grass, oversized sunglasses, and a faint look of regret. She nodded politely, then sat on a blanket and began setting up a small ink set with barely a sound.

Evie muttered, "One of them is emotionally repressed. I just haven't worked out which."

Just as Jules launched into a monologue about "dandelion consciousness," Beatrice Simmons bustled onto the field like a burst of warm vanilla.

"Hope no one minds," she said brightly, holding up a cake tin, "but I made oat-and-blackberry slices. They're technically part of a study I'm doing on edible textures, but I won't be offended if anyone just eats them for fun."

Beatrice wore wide-legged corduroy trousers, a mustard-coloured jumper with a slightly flour-dusted shoulder, and a scarf printed with teapots and tiny cats. Her glasses slipped slightly as she squinted into the light, but she smiled at everyone like she'd known them forever.

Jules took a slice immediately. "This is *vibrationally aligned*."

Claudia took none.

Evie snagged two and whispered to Annabel, "She's either secretly a genius or just too kind to survive this group."

Annabel smiled. "Both, maybe."

Persephone circled Beatrice once, sniffed the air, and walked away with obvious suspicion. She did *not* trust baked goods that weren't offered directly.

***

Then came Elena Halberd.

She walked in like she was used to being watched. Not with vanity — with vigilance.

Loose linen. Soft-soled shoes.

No jewellery. Her dark hair was pinned up in a loose twist, strands escaping like they had better things to do.

She nodded to Basil. Briefly. Chose the furthest corner of the meadow.

Evie leaned over. "She's either heartbreak in human form or here to bury a body."

Annabel murmured, "Or both."

Elena painted without preamble.

No pleasantries. Just brush to paper, a small glass jar of water at her elbow and a quiet intensity that pushed the air away around her.

***

The meadow filled with gentle rustling. Birdsong. Brushes on paper. Occasional sighs of creative frustration.

Annabel tried to paint a coneflower. It came out... confused.

She tried again. This time, she focused on how the petals leaned. The way they didn't beg to be noticed, but still were. It was better.

She looked up just as Elena dipped her brush with fingers that trembled — just slightly.

Claudia saw it too.

Neither of them said a word.

***

Persephone stalked past Jules, who yelped when she stepped on his palette, then strolled directly into Claudia's lap like she was inspecting a suspect. Claudia froze.

Evie, watching from the shade, laughed. "She always knows who needs unsettling."

***

When the class ended, Basil declared it "a triumph of soul meeting season."

People packed up slowly.

Elena didn't speak to anyone. Just wiped her brush, folded her chair, and disappeared between the tall grass.

Claudia lingered a moment longer, staring at Elena's empty spot. Then she too walked away — her palette perfectly clean.

Annabel closed her sketchbook. It wasn't her best work. But it was hers.

Persephone leapt into her arms, purring once — like a punctuation mark.

Tomorrow, they'd paint at the old chapel.

And somehow, Annabel already knew: something there would not be still.

Chapter 2

The ruins of the chapel stood like broken teeth against the skyline, softened only by ivy and time.

It wasn't much — three standing walls, a crooked stone arch where the door had once been, and a floor overrun with moss and wild violets. But it was quiet. Still. A place where sound softened and breath slowed.

Annabel stood just inside the boundary wall, sketchbook under one arm, watching as light filtered through the open roof. The sun scattered through the cracks like spilled gold.

Persephone wound between her feet, tail flicking, as if inspecting the sacred geometry of the stones for her own mysterious reasons.

***

Beatrice appeared with her usual thermos and a smile that didn't know how to be anything else.

"Oh, I know this place," she said, stepping over a cracked flagstone. "I baked for a wedding here, years ago. Well — it started here, anyway."

Evie looked up from her pencil case. "In the ruins?"

"It was very fashionable at the time. Rustic romance. Flowers in jam jars. Crumbling symbolism."

"And?" Annabel prompted, already amused.

Beatrice sighed. "A roof tile came loose halfway through the vows. Landed directly on the wedding cake. The top tier slid off like it had somewhere better to be. I had to patch it with glacé cherries and hope no one noticed."

Evie cackled. "Was the bride furious?"

"She was wearing heels in a field. She was already furious."

***

The group settled in slowly.

Claudia chose a shadowed corner near a twisted window. Her strokes were sharp, deliberate, and silent.

Jules sat dramatically at a broken pew, one foot up like he was posing for a Renaissance allegory. He stared up at the ruined ceiling and said, "This place is giving me rebirth energy."

Nell, cardigan even bigger today, quietly chose a patch of wild thyme and unpacked her charcoal set with no fanfare.

Elena arrived last. She didn't greet anyone. Just nodded once at Basil, then set herself up near what had once been the altar.

Annabel watched her carefully.

Her composition was immediate. Confident. Her lines were clean, her washes subtle. But something felt missing.

It was beautiful — but it didn't breathe.

***

Near the archway, Beatrice had perched on a stool beside Basil, a sketchpad balanced on her lap. She wasn't drawing — not yet.

"I remember her earlier work," she said softly. "One painting I saw — a woodland path — felt like it had teeth. I couldn't stop looking at it. It scared me. In the best way."

Basil hummed, sipping something that definitely wasn't herbal tea. "Yes. That was her wild phase. A burst of passion. Untamed. She painted with risk back then."

"What happened?" Beatrice asked.

"She learned to be careful."

Jules leaned in from across the broken window. "She's not gone. She's just still. Like Monet in winter."

Evie, nearby, leaned over to Annabel. "They're all saying the same thing. She lost it."

Annabel watched Elena dip her brush again, her hand perfectly steady. The painting was emerging in soft blues and greys — technically flawless. Emotionally silent.

"She's not lost," Annabel murmured. "She's plateaued."

And no one who called themselves an artist liked to admit that.

***

The late sun shifted as they worked, casting long, warped shadows across the mossy floor. Dust sparkled in the air like slow-falling confetti.

Annabel had chosen a stone near the wall, where she could sketch a shattered arch dripping with ivy. The vines framed the opening like nature trying to stitch the ruin back together.

She let her brush drift. Soft strokes. Loose lines. No pressure. It felt... nice.

Persephone had disappeared somewhere among the ferns growing out of the wall. Hopefully not hunting anything sacred.

***

Midway through the session, Elena's hand paused. Only for a second.

She pressed the back of her wrist to her temple, then bent forward as if to reach for her water jar — but missed. Her fingers hesitated just above the tin, then drew back.

She didn't look at anyone. Didn't speak.

Claudia, two meters away, paused mid-stroke.

She didn't say anything either. But her brush remained suspended in the air for a moment too long — like it was waiting to hear something only she could hear.

***

Evie had perched on a chunk of collapsed stone nearby, sketching a half-finished window as if it had insulted her personally.

"She doesn't look well," she murmured.

Annabel glanced up. Elena was working again — as if nothing had happened — but her posture was off. Shoulders tight. Jaw set.

"It's hot," Annabel said. "Maybe she's dehydrated."

"Maybe." Evie frowned. "She doesn't *drink*, though. Or eat. Or blink."

"Maybe she's just focused."

"Or haunted."

***

As the session wrapped up, Basil did a slow, murmured circuit, offering poetic feedback that sounded mostly like botanical dream logic. Jules was lying flat on his back, whispering something about transcendence to a passing crow. Nell packed up silently, brushing dust from her lap with long, delicate fingers.

Beatrice poured tea from her thermos and offered Annabel a biscuit. It was, somehow, still warm.

"I don't think Elena will stay the whole retreat," she said quietly.

Annabel looked over. Elena was folding her brushes with delicate precision. Every movement slow. Measured.

"Why not?"

Bea shrugged. "Because someone that is tightly wound either snaps or disappears. And I've seen both."

***

Persephone emerged at the edge of the chapel, carrying a *perfectly square piece of weathered paper* in her mouth.

She dropped it on Annabel's shoe like an offering. Or a dare.

Annabel bent down. The edge was torn. The paper was thick — high-quality — and marked with a faint stain of... ochre?

She turned it over.

Just the corner of a sketch. A style she almost recognised. A signature that was cut off — just **IV**...

Claudia stood nearby, closing her sketchbook.

Their eyes met.

And Claudia smiled — just slightly.

It wasn't a nice smile.

Chapter 3

The lake by Larchwood was glassy, green, and perfect.

Too perfect.

Annabel sat on a blanket near the edge, brush in hand, eyes tracing the reflections in the water. Dragonflies zipped over the surface like they had somewhere else to be. The trees on the far bank leaned in like gossiping old women.

Persephone stood at the shoreline and looked out with open disdain.

Then she turned, stalked three steps into the sand, and dug an absolutely furious hole, flinging dry earth with aggressive precision.

Evie watched. "She's already bored of the aesthetic."

"She doesn't like still water," Annabel murmured.

"She told you that, did she?"

"With her entire soul."

Persephone finished her excavation, buried a twig like it had offended her, and vanished into the reeds.

***

The group had spread out.

Basil had declared the site *"a visual metaphor for artistic honesty"*, then disappeared behind a willow with a flask of something that smelled like regret.

Jules had removed his shoes and was painting with his toes.

Nell, across from him, was quietly sketching. Her cardigan today was navy. Her sunglasses were back on. Her expression was unreadable.

Claudia sat under a tree, painting reeds with obsessive focus — every line perfect, clinical, almost cold.

And Elena... was on the dock.

Sitting cross-legged, her water jar beside her, her sketchbook balanced like an altar offering.

Her painting took shape fast — bold outlines, clean washes, exact shading.

It was beautiful. But it didn't feel like anything.

Then her brush paused.

She blinked. Shifted slightly. Her hand trembled for a second — not a lot, but enough.

She reached for her jar… and missed it by an inch.

Claudia, under the tree, stopped painting mid-stroke.

Annabel saw both.

Neither of them said a word.

***

Beatrice arrived, bouncing slightly on the path, with a tin in one hand and a travel mug in the other.

"Raspberry muffins," she called. "Fresh from the oven. I felt like someone might need sweetness today."

Evie immediately stood. "You always know. It's either witchcraft or intuition, and I respect both."

Bea passed out muffins like communion. When she reached Elena, the painter barely looked up.

"No, thank you," Elena said softly, her voice distant, eyes on the water.

Bea frowned slightly, but moved on.

***

Later, during the break, Jules wandered off to "commune with reflection" (Evie translated: "pee behind a tree"). He left his kit unattended.

Evie, naturally curious, peeked.

Inside, tucked under sketchpads, was a *small tin* — unlabelled, but with a faint smear of *rusty orange pigment* around the lid.

Persephone reappeared *at that exact moment*, sitting behind Evie like a spectral witness.

"She's looming," Evie said, lifting the tin. "You see this? She sees this. Everyone sees this."

Annabel frowned. "That's not a colour Basil's given us."

"Could be cadmium. Could be evil."

"Let's not accuse Jules of attempted poisoning."

"Too late. I've named the tin *Suspicious Spice*."

Persephone gently swatted it off the edge of the bag. It rolled toward Annabel, who caught it mid-spin.

She looked at the smear again. Something about the texture didn't seem... quite right.

***

As the session wound down, Basil emerged to call them in for "communal reflection." Only half the group obeyed. Elena stayed on the dock.

Annabel passed behind her on the way to pack up.

She glanced at the painting.

It was the far side of the lake — trees, water, stone. Beautifully rendered. But the colour palette was wrong. Too pale. Off-tone. Emotionless.

And... oddly familiar.

Annabel narrowed her eyes.

She'd seen something like this before. Not here. In a book. A gallery catalogue.

By Isolde Voss.

Persephone trotted out of the trees with something dangling from her mouth.

It was a ribbon — pale blue, paint-streaked, frayed at one end.

She dropped it neatly at Claudia's feet, then sat and began cleaning her paw.

Claudia stared at it for a beat too long.

Then, wordlessly, she picked it up, folded it, and slid it into her sketchbook.

Annabel caught the moment — just as Claudia looked up and met her gaze.

And smiled.

Not a friendly smile.

Just... a *knowing one.*

Chapter 4

The barn smelled of old hay, dust, and rain.

Annabel stepped inside and immediately understood why Basil had called it *"an intimate setting for focused observation."*

Translation: *drafty, dim, and full of vibes.*

The group trickled in slowly, peeling off coats and shaking out umbrellas. Rain tapped gently against the old windows. The lighting was soft and grey — the kind that made everything feel slightly more haunted than it needed to be.

Evie unrolled her mat and squinted up at the rafters. "If a bat flies into my water cup, I'm taking that as a sign to change careers."

***

Persephone had already claimed the most structurally questionable beam and was lying across it like a gargoyle with opinions.

Claudia was the first to set up. Again.

She chose the far corner — quiet, shadowed. Her setup was precise: brushes in order, palette clean, sketchbook unopened.

Elena arrived last. Again.

She looked... drained. Not just tired — *hollow.* Like someone painting out of obligation, not obsession. She nodded vaguely at Basil, ignored Jules entirely, and took the seat closest to the window.

Basil paced slowly down the centre of the room like a priest preparing for creative communion.

"Here, we remove the distractions of nature to meet the rawness of form," he intoned.

Evie muttered, "Sounds like a fancy way to say 'bad lighting.'"

***

The session began.

Annabel worked on a still life — a vase of wildflowers left by someone optimistic. She watched as the others quietly fell into rhythm.

Except Claudia.

She wasn't painting.

She was... *mixing.*

Her hands moved precisely, quietly. She scraped a *tiny amount of pigment* from a tin — one not on Basil's materials list — and swirled it into a separate jar of water. A dull ochre, like dried leaves and bitterness.

She dipped a test strip, studied the colour, frowned.

Then she tucked the jar behind her box, just barely out of sight.

Annabel didn't say anything.

But she noted the action.

And the distance between Claudia and Elena's seat.

***

The rain thickened. Shadows deepened.

Jules attempted something abstract and large and accidentally flung red pigment across Nell's paper. She didn't speak — just moved to a different bench.

Elena winced. Not at the mess. At the sound of the splatter.

Beatrice handed out warm oat cookies like a therapy session.

Persephone descended from her beam to accept one, then sniffed Claudia's water jar and hissed quietly.

Claudia gently nudged her away with the back of her sketchbook.

Not angry. Just... firm.

Evie watched it all like someone collecting secrets for a rainy day.

***

At the end of the session, Annabel caught sight of Elena's latest piece.

It was a still life of the vase — perfectly captured. Soft shadows. Precise stems. Not a petal out of place.

But next to it, Claudia's version was different.

Less literal. But alive.

There was energy in the strokes. Movement. A flare of colour Annabel hadn't seen in the original scene.

And a hint of ochre in the shadows.

***

As they packed up, Elena brushed past Claudia with her sketchpad tucked under her arm.

Neither of them spoke.

But Claudia glanced down — and for one split second, her hand hovered over the jar she'd hidden.

Just long enough for Persephone to hop up onto the bench and place a paw directly on the lid.

Claudia froze. Then she smiled.

Only Annabel saw it. And it wasn't a smile of joy.

It was a smile of *knowing.*

Chapter 5

The Hare & Hound had seen every kind of local drama: wedding toasts, funeral toasts, football fights, quiet divorces, and once, a goat on a Tuesday. Today, it welcomed something new — *artists.*

The pub's thick stone walls trapped the smell of roast potatoes and damp coats. A fire crackled in the hearth. Locals pretended not to be interested in the new arrivals, while tilting their hearing aids and teapots just slightly toward the long table near the window.

Annabel, Evie, and Persephone claimed the corner booth like seasoned regulars. Persephone immediately leapt onto the red-padded bench and curled up as if she'd booked the table under her name.

"She's acting like she owns the place," Annabel murmured. "She probably does," said Evie. "The real mystery in this village is how no one's realized she's in charge."

***

The others trickled in.

Basil, scarf still somehow dry, claimed the head of the long table and launched straight into an anecdote about expressionism and the ethics of goat cheese.

Jules and Nell sat opposite each other, mid-cold-war, with Jules talking louder than necessary and Nell stirring her tea like it was the drink's fault she was here.

Beatrice arrived carrying a small pastry box, smiling warmly as if nothing in the world could surprise her — not even this odd, atmospheric crowd.

Claudia came in last, shoulders slightly hunched, hair wind-tossed. She scanned the room, spotted an empty chair at the far end of the table, and slid into it without a word.

***

The locals were already there, of course.

Colin Denby, in his usual tweed waistcoat, held court at the bar like a man waiting to be asked for wisdom.

Mrs. Broom had taken over the table nearest the fireplace with a stack of crossword books and a listening face.

And Nora from the bookshop, perched by the window, sipped a sherry with the deliberate slowness of someone who didn't want to miss a single syllable.

None of them looked over when the artists came in.

But every one of them was absolutely *listening.*

***

Annabel sipped her elderflower cordial, watching it all unfold with quiet intensity. Evie was beside her, already halfway through the drinks' menu — metaphorically, if not physically.

"Ten quid says this ends in either tears or philosophical fisticuffs," Evie whispered.

"My money's on cryptic insults and someone storming out before dessert."

Persephone stretched; one paw elegantly draped across the table like she was waiting to order wine.

***

Lunch arrived in waves — shepherd's pies, ploughman's platters, one suspiciously beige vegan curry, and *Beatrice's famous pear and walnut tartlets*, which were unwrapped and offered around like sacred scrolls.

"I brought these just in case anyone needed grounding," Beatrice said, placing one carefully in front of Elena.

Elena blinked, looked at the tartlet like she wasn't quite sure what it was, and gave a faint smile.

"No, thank you," she said. Her voice was quiet. Her hands were pale.

Beatrice, undeterred, moved on.

"She's not well," she murmured to Annabel and Evie as she slid into the booth beside them. "More than tired, I'd say."

"She missed her water jar earlier," Annabel said. "Almost like she couldn't see it."

"Or forgot where it was," Evie added, frowning.

"Bit pale, that one," Colin muttered from the bar. "Like a candle about to snuff itself."

Mrs. Broom didn't look up. "She's an artist, Colin. They *like* looking haunted. Makes the work seem deep."

"I'm just saying, people who stop eating at a pub lunch are usually either dying or lying."

Nora delicately flipped a page of her tiny notepad. "Or both."

***

Nearby, Jules launched into a story that involved the phrase *"emotional lineage of colour theory."*

Nell cut in; voice flat. "You said she'd be gone by now."

Everyone at the table paused.

Jules flushed. "I meant gone as in... evolving. *Metaphorically.*"

Evie leaned toward Annabel. "Did he just admit to scheduling a disappearance?"

"Let's not get too murder-y over soup."

"Too late."

***

Annabel opened her bag to grab her notebook — and found *Evie's hand already in it.*

"I brought it," Evie said, pulling out the pigment tin.

Persephone immediately sat up and *stared* at it like it owed her money.

Annabel's breath caught. "Here?"

Evie shrugged. "It's just a tin."

Beatrice leaned closer. "May I?"

Evie passed it to her. Persephone followed the motion like a Wimbledon umpire.

Bea turned the tin in her fingers. "Nope. Not from our set. I helped Basil prep the kits — this one's older. Definitely not one of the 'safe stock.'"

"Safe stock?" Annabel asked.

"You know — non-toxic, student grade, locally sourced. Basil insisted.

This one's... someone's personal addition."

"Yours?"

Beatrice shook her head. "I don't touch that tone. Makes shadows too muddy. And it flakes when it dries."

Evie nudged Annabel. "So, it's not just ugly. It's dangerous."

Persephone batted it once, then placed a single paw on the lid.

***

Claudia stood.

She hadn't spoken once the entire lunch.

As she passed their booth, Persephone slid off the bench and trotted into her path — with something in her mouth.

A pale blue ribbon. Paint-streaked. Frayed.

Jules raised his voice about colour harmony just as Nell put down her fork and said, "Please stop."

Colin leaned over to Nora. "Never trust a man in linen who talks like a thesaurus."

Nora didn't respond. She was staring at Claudia — just as Persephone laid the ribbon on the floor.

Claudia stopped.

Her eyes dropped to the floor. The ribbon.

Then rose slowly to meet Annabel's.

A long moment passed.

Then, softly — as if speaking to herself — Claudia said:

"You've got a good eye. That's dangerous in a village like this." And then she was gone.

***

Persephone curled back up in the booth.

The ribbon stayed where it had fallen — like a whisper someone hadn't meant to hear.

Chapter 6

The trees leaned in as if they were listening.

Witch's Hollow didn't appear on most maps. You had to know the right path from the north hedgerow, past the leaning stone with the carved spiral, through two fields and a thicket that looked like it hadn't been walked through in a hundred years.

And then suddenly — the trees opened.

The glade was still. Too still.

The clearing had a soft moss floor and tangled roots like sleeping animals. Ferns lined the edges. A ring of old stones — not quite a circle — hugged the centre like forgotten chairs.

No birdsong. No wind. Just breath.

Annabel tightened her scarf.

Persephone, already ahead, padded toward the far end of the hollow with the air of a creature returning to somewhere she'd ruled in a previous life.

***

They'd heard about the place at the Hare & Hound the night before — *almost by accident.*

Annabel had only mentioned the name once, and suddenly the pub had gone oddly quiet. Like someone had hit mute.

***

At the pub, the night before, Colin Denby, nursing something dark and ancient-looking in a chipped glass:

"Witch's Hollow, is it? Haven't heard that name said out loud in a while. Funny how sound disappears there. Things too."

Mrs. Broom, without looking up from her knitting: "You know someone once found a scarecrow in the trees. Upside down. Kids, maybe. Or not."

Nora, quietly from the corner, sherry in hand: "Place was named after a woman who vanished. No trial. No body. Just an empty cabin with the kettle still warm. Folk stopped walking their dogs that way after that."

Persephone, asleep on the bar, opened one eye. Watched. Didn't blink.

***

Now, with her boots damp and the trees whispering overhead, Annabel understood.

This was not just a location.

It was *a mood.*

***

"Where *is* everyone?" Evie asked, glancing over her shoulder. "Weren't we supposed to meet here at the hollow?"

"They're behind us. Basil was monologuing about bark textures."

"I'm not emotionally prepared to be murdered by a metaphor."

***

Claudia was the first to arrive after them. She stepped into the glade like she was entering a chapel. Her eyes flicked to the ring of stones. She chose a seat on the far side. Unpacked her brushes.

Didn't speak.

Jules and Nell appeared next — unusually quiet. Jules muttered something about "ritualistic energy" and then tripped over a root.

Nell didn't help him up.

Beatrice followed, carrying a flask of spiced tea and a tin that jingled when she walked.

"Fig and almond biscuits. For bravery."

Annabel took one gratefully.

"Where's Elena?" she asked.

Beatrice looked around. "She wasn't at breakfast."

Jules frowned. "She said she was going for a walk before class. To clear her head."

Claudia didn't look up.

"She's always going for walks."

***

Basil arrived last. Flushed. Enthusiastic. Oblivious.

He clapped his hands together.

"Let the trees guide your instinct. If you feel something ancient... paint it."

Persephone sat in the middle of the stone circle and yawned.

***

They painted in near silence.

Even Evie didn't speak much.

The quiet settled like a second skin. Thoughts moved slower here. Colours looked richer. Annabel found herself painting not what she saw — but what she *felt*.

Roots.

Memory.

The absence of birds.

But the longer they painted... the more obvious the *absence* became.

Elena wasn't just late.

She was *gone*.

***

It was Claudia who said it first — just before they began packing.

"Has anyone checked the path back?"

Jules stood. "She said she'd meet us."

Beatrice frowned. "She wouldn't miss a session."

Annabel looked down at her palette.

One of the colours — a soft greyish blue — was missing. The pan was *wet.* Recently used.

Evie crouched, running her fingers through the moss.

There were boot prints.

Two sets.

Leading in.

None leading out.

Persephone rose slowly. Tail stiff.

She turned toward the edge of the woods — and hissed.

Chapter 7

The wind changed sometime after lunch.

It came down through the trees in Witch's Hollow like a sigh — low, cold, and full of things unsaid. Annabel felt it brush her skin and wondered why the birds hadn't come back.

The group had lingered for almost an hour after Claudia's remark. They'd searched the path twice, circled the glade, even shouted Elena's name into the trees — once, loudly. Once, a little afraid.

Nothing. No sign of her. No answer.

***

By the time they'd packed up and made their way back to the village, the Hollow behind them felt heavier. Like the trees were closing the door.

Persephone kept looking back.

***

The pub was quieter than usual at dusk. A few locals glanced up when they entered, and then quickly looked away — which, in Firling, was the equivalent of a scream.

Mrs. Broom was the first to say it.

"You're short one."

Annabel nodded. "We... haven't seen her since this morning."

Colin, from his usual stool:

"Place like that swallows you whole if it wants. I said it."

Nora, from behind a book: "Some disappear by choice. Some by invitation."

Evie ordered tea. With whisky in it.

Persephone climbed onto the bar and lay down in a loaf of feline judgment.

***

Basil, looking uncharacteristically frazzled, tried to reassure them.

"She's done this before," he said. "Disappears to paint in private. Connect with the landscape. Elena's a... *solitary soul.*"

"Solitary soul or not," Beatrice said softly, "she left her kit. And her food."

"And her coat," Nell added. "She always wears that coat."

That landed like a stone in the middle of the table.

***

Evie returned from the bar with a second round of "tea" and dropped into the seat beside Annabel.

"She's really just... gone, huh?" she muttered. "No note. No coat. No drama. That's almost worse."

Across the room, Nora Greaves closed her book and stood. Slowly. Carefully.

She walked past their table, then paused just long enough to place her sherry glass down.

"Strange thing about disappearances," she said softly, eyes not quite meeting theirs,

"is how easily we forget who *wasn't* there when they happened."

Annabel turned. "What do you mean?"

Nora offered a thin smile.

"You all searched. Called. Worried."

A pause.

"I don't remember hearing anyone say where *Claudia* had gone."

She walked away without another word, cardigan trailing like punctuation.

Evie blinked.

"...Okay. That was either the softest mic drops in history or I need to reread my entire life."

Annabel didn't answer.

Because suddenly... she wasn't sure where Claudia had been either.

***

The light had gone grey and still at Honeystone Cottage.

Annabel sat with her sketchbook open but untouched, Persephone curled tight against her side like a shadow with fur.

Evie returned from the kitchen with mugs and news.

"Jules is messaging her. No reply."

"Did she leave anything at the Hollow?" Annabel asked.

"No one saw her drop anything. But..." Evie hesitated. "Basil said there was a piece of paper folded into her palette. He didn't open it. Thought it was a reference image or something."

Annabel stood up immediately.

***

The two of them returned under fading light at Witch's Hollow.

Evie was muttering about horror movie logic and dying first, but Annabel's steps were certain.

They found the spot where Elena had been painting. Her palette was still there, tucked under a rock for weight. A few leaves had settled over it.

Annabel brushed them aside.

There, folded neatly, was a slip of heavy paper — thick, watermarked, the kind real artists used.

She unfolded it.

No painting.

Just a few words, scrawled in a looping, unfamiliar hand:

"*I found the truth. But not where I thought it was.*"

***

Persephone, who had followed them soundlessly, stared into the trees.

A second later, she let out the softest growl Annabel had ever heard her make.

Evie exhaled slowly. "That's not ideal."

Chapter 8

The studio was nothing like Annabel expected.

She'd imagined something grand — all tall ceilings, light, and mood. Maybe canvases leaning against the walls, the smell of turpentine in the air.

But the space above the bakery was *small, spare, and oddly quiet.*

The landlord had given Basil the spare key when Elena failed to return. "For safety reasons," he'd said, but hadn't asked too many questions.

Basil was meant to come. He hadn't.

Annabel didn't wait.

The staircase creaked beneath her boots. Persephone padded ahead, tail high, as if she'd rented the place last week and was simply checking in.

Annabel hesitated at the top.

The door opened with a whisper.

The room inside was still.

Natural light filtered through a skylight. The walls were painted pale grey, and the furniture was minimal — a stool, a narrow table, a chair with a coat still draped over it.

Elena's coat.

Annabel stepped inside.

It smelled faintly of citrus and something older. Not paint. Something... dry.

The room was clean. Too clean.

***

Canvases leaned in one corner. Not dozens — just four.

Three of them were finished. One was covered with a cloth.

She moved toward them, slowly. Persephone sniffed the edges of a crate and sneezed once, disdainfully.

***

The top three paintings were... fine.

Beautiful, even.

Soft scenes. Lake reflections. A wildflower meadow. The chapel ruins.

But... again... no fire. No feeling.

The brushstrokes were smooth and deliberate. Controlled. *Contained.*

Annabel's heart started to beat faster — not because of what she saw, but because of what she *didn't.*

There was *no sketchbook.*

No thumbnails. No colour tests.

No open palette.

No coffee mug.

No mess.

And artists were *messy.*

***

She pulled the cloth off the final canvas.

It was unfinished.

Not half-done, but *halted.* Like the painter had stopped mid-thought.

Dark lines. A figure. A glade.

Witch's Hollow.

Annabel's fingers curled slightly at her sides.

This painting felt different.

Like it had *started to say something real.*

She turned, suddenly chilled.

Persephone was staring at a chest of drawers near the window — silent and stiff, tail low.

Annabel approached.

There was a smear of something on the handle. Dry pigment?

She pulled it open.

Inside: sketchbooks. Six of them.

Stacked. Sealed with elastic.

She pulled the top one out, flipped it open — and gasped.

***

The sketches were sharper. Bolder. *Fearless.*

But not unfamiliar.

These were similar to the style Elena had used *when she first became famous.*

Back when people said she painted like lightning on paper. Back when her work had *bite.*

Annabel turned the page. Another sketch — twisted ivy over stone, sketched in ink and shadowed in burnt umber. The lines moved. Dared.

She remembered the fragment Persephone had brought to her days ago.

She checked the corner.

There it was — signed, faintly:

"I. V."

Annabel's fingers tightened around the edge of the page.

Whatever this was...

It hadn't started with Elena.

*****

A soft sound behind her.

Not loud. Just... a shift.

She turned.

No one was there.

But the coat on the chair — the one Elena always wore — had fallen to the floor.

*****

Persephone growled.

Chapter 9

Annabel didn't sleep.

She tried — twice — curling up beneath her quilt while Persephone kept vigil at the windowsill like a gargoyle with opinions. But her mind spun too fast.

The sketchbook still sat on her desk, spine cracked, corners frayed. She hadn't opened it again.

Not yet.

***

By morning, the sky was pale and fogged. Rain misted the garden like a secret. The coneflowers looked tired. The black-eyed Susans had stopped reaching for the light.

Evie wandered into the kitchen wearing two different socks and no remorse.

"You're making murder-face," she said, reaching for toast. "Tell me everything."

Annabel told her.
About the studio.
The paintings.
The *style.*
The signature.
Evie listened. Quiet for once.
Her toast went untouched.

When Annabel finished, she leaned back and said, "You realise what this means, right?"

"That Elena copied someone?"

"That *Elena was never the artist we thought she was.*"

A long pause.

Persephone blinked slowly. She already knew.

***

Annabel stood and opened the sketchbook again.

She flipped past a crumbling spine to the next page.

There — a portrait. Not finished. But Annabel recognised the curve of the cheek, the sharpness of the eyes.

Elena.

Drawn not as a friend.

Not as a peer.

But like *a subject.*

Observed. Studied.

Possibly... claimed.

***

Evie frowned.

"So that's why Claudia's always watching her."

"She recognises the work."

Annabel didn't answer.

She didn't have to.

***

The knock came mid-morning.

Soft. Precise. Two taps.

Annabel opened the door to Claudia.

Hair damp from the mist. A sketchbook under one arm. No smile.

"I need to speak with you," she said. "Privately."

***

Evie stood. "Nope. We're not doing any *alone in the murder fog* scenes today."

Claudia's gaze flicked to her, unamused.

"It's not about Elena," she said.

That was, of course, a lie.

***

Annabel hesitated. Then stepped aside.

Claudia entered, moved like smoke, and took the chair nearest the fire. She looked tired.

Not dramatically — just worn around the edges. Like something she'd been carrying was finally digging through the fabric. She didn't speak right away.

Persephone sat on the hearth. Watching.

***

Finally, Claudia opened her sketchbook.

On the first page: a drawing. A chapel. Stone and ivy. Shadows that bled across the paper like regret.

Annabel's breath caught.

It was almost identical to the one she'd found in the studio. But this one was signed.

Clearly.

"Isolde Voss."

Claudia closed the book.

"My mother drew that in 1986. Elena took the sketch. Painted it. Entered it in a competition. Won."

Her voice didn't shake. But her hands did.

"She said they'd collaborated. But no one ever saw the original sketch again."

***

Evie leaned against the kitchen counter. "So, you came here to what — scare her? Expose her?"

Claudia met her gaze. "I came here to *witness her unravel.* That was enough."

Annabel felt something twist inside.

"But she disappeared," she said softly.

Claudia didn't blink.

"I know."

***

A long silence.

Then Claudia stood.

"She was sick before she arrived," she said. "I didn't have to do anything."

And with that, she left.

***

The door closed.

Persephone hissed — not loud. Just a little. Like punctuation.

Evie looked at Annabel.

"Well," she said, "I guess we're *definitely* part of this now."

Annabel said nothing.

But she opened the sketchbook one more time.

And turned the page.

Chapter 10

It rained through the night.

Not a storm — just the kind of steady, whispering downpour that made everything feel muffled and old.

By morning, the world outside the cottage was grey and wet. The garden looked bruised. The earth smelled like secrets.

Annabel sat at the kitchen table, Persephone curled beside her, sketching absentminded spirals onto a page already too full of thoughts.

Evie placed a mug beside her and said, "It's started."

Annabel looked up. "What?"

Evie raised an eyebrow. "The *falling apart.*"

∗∗∗

Basil had changed the day's session to indoors at the village hall. The weather, he claimed, wasn't "artistically generous." In truth, everyone looked rattled.

Even Basil's scarf was uneven. That was a sign.

∗∗∗

Beatrice brought in a tray of jam muffins and kept her voice calm. But she kept glancing at the door — and not in a hopeful way.

Jules was pacing.

Nell was silent.

Claudia sat in the corner, sketchbook open, back perfectly straight.

Basil kept checking his phone.

No one said Elena's name.

***

Then Jules broke.

"I don't care what anyone says," he snapped. "Someone knows what happened to her."

The room froze.

"People don't just vanish," he continued, voice rising. "Not without planning. Not without help. Or... or *motive*."

He looked straight at Claudia.

***

Annabel felt her stomach knot.

Evie didn't move.

Claudia didn't blink.

"I know what you think," Jules said. "We all know. The gallery gossip. The whispers. You said nothing until she disappeared."

Claudia's voice was quiet.

"I said nothing because it wasn't the right time."

Beatrice spoke gently. "But now is?"

Claudia looked up. "She's gone. And *you're all still pretending* her art meant something."

***

A long silence.

Persephone, perched on the windowsill, growled.

***

Nell, for the first time, spoke.

"She told me once," she said slowly, "that her hands stopped listening to her."

Everyone turned.

"I thought it was just metaphor. But maybe... maybe she knew something was wrong."

Jules muttered, "She knew she was losing it."

Basil stood suddenly.

"That's enough."

His voice echoed.

"She was still brilliant. Still working. She needed time. Not judgment."

"Then why didn't you *say* she was sick?" Evie asked.

Basil's mouth opened. Closed.

No answer.

***

Annabel stood. Quietly. Carefully.

"I went to her studio," she said.

The room turned.

"I found her coat. Her unfinished painting. A sketchbook with someone else's name on it."

Claudia said nothing.

Beatrice whispered, "Whose name?"

Annabel looked down at her notebook.

Then back up.

"*Isolde Voss.*"

Nell gasped.

Jules looked sick.

And Claudia finally spoke. "She didn't deserve that name. Not after what she did."

***

No one moved.

Outside, the rain fell harder.

Persephone jumped from the sill and trotted to Annabel's side, tail stiff, ears forward.

Chapter 11

They returned to Witch's Hollow before anyone else.

No group session today — Basil had "suspended all creative gathering" until Elena was "located or mourned."

Annabel wasn't ready for either.

The Hollow was quieter than before. The kind of quiet that pressed against the skin.

Persephone walked ahead, tail high, ears twitching. She didn't hesitate — just moved, determined, toward the north edge of the glade.

Annabel followed.

Evie muttered behind her, "If she leads us to a body, I'm making her wear a bell."

***

They reached a cluster of mossy stones tangled in ivy.

Persephone stopped.

She sat.

She stared.

Annabel's eyes followed hers.

And saw *the glint*.

Something metal. Half-buried beneath roots.

She crouched and brushed it away — gently, carefully.

A small silver tin, square, ornate, cold.

Evie stepped closer.

"What is it?"

Annabel opened it.

Inside: *a brooch.*

Simple. Elegant. A small enamel painting at the centre — a chapel wrapped in ivy.

Annabel's fingers tingled.

It was the *same scene* from the sketch fragment.

The *same brush style.*

But not Elena's.

On the back: a faint engraving.

Worn, but still visible.

"*To I.V., with reverence. — E.*"

***

Annabel went very still.

Evie looked at her. "So, Elena knew. She *knew.*"

"She kept this." Annabel's voice was thin. "She buried it."

"Or someone *buried it for her.*"

They both looked up at the trees.

Nothing moved.

But it *felt* like something was nearby.

***

Back at the cottage, the fire was low and the fog had returned.

Annabel sat at the kitchen table with the objects laid out in front of her like quiet accusations.

The brooch.

The pigment tin.

The sketch fragment.

The note.

The sketchbook.

Evie placed a mug of something dark and cinnamon-spiced in front of her.

"You're making detective face," she said.

Annabel didn't look up.

Evie sat across from her, folded her arms, and said, "Let's go full Miss Marple."

***

Annabel nodded slowly. "We know Elena knew about Isolde. That brooch isn't a theft. It's... *reverence.*"

"Guilt," Evie said. "Or worship. Or both."

"She admired her. Maybe even loved her work. But she still took it. Used it."

"Doesn't matter what you feel if your name ends up in the museum and hers doesn't."

***

Persephone batted the pigment tin off the table.

Evie caught it midair. "This tin still creeps me out. But maybe it's not poison."

Annabel blinked. "Then what?"

"Maybe it's a decoy. Planted. Or something older that was never meant to be found."

Annabel flipped open the sketchbook. The portrait. Elena's eyes. The brushstroke like accusation.

"She was poisoned, Evie. Or something close. And I don't think Claudia did it."

Evie leaned in. "Then who?"

***

A pause.

Then, softly: "Someone who's not in the room."

Evie's eyes narrowed. "Like... a legacy fixer?"

Annabel nodded. "Someone who's *managing the story.* Not just hiding the past — *cleaning it.*"

***

Persephone leapt onto the table and planted herself directly across the sketchbook. She flicked her tail once, decisively.

Evie whispered, "Cat says case's still open."

Annabel wrote a single sentence at the top of her notebook: *We are not alone in this story.*

She stared at it for a long time.

Then she whispered:

"And they're not done yet."

Chapter 12

The bookshop didn't have a bell.

It didn't need one.

Nora always knew when someone walked in.

Annabel barely had time to close the door behind her before she heard:

"You've come looking for names."

***

Nora stood behind the till, arranging bookmarks like they were tarot cards.

She looked up, serene as always, and added, "It's always names in the end.

Even when people think they're chasing truth."

Annabel blinked. "I didn't—"

"I know."

Nora smiled.

***

Persephone slinked in behind her and leapt silently onto a shelf of Gothic novels, knocking *Wuthering Heights* sideways without a shred of remorse.

***

Annabel moved slowly through the shop, past poetry and memoirs and a table labelled *"Read with Regret."*

"I wanted to ask," she said, "about... Isolde Voss."

Nora didn't flinch.

"I was afraid of that."

***

Silence curled in like fog.

Annabel didn't push. Just waited.

Finally, Nora nodded toward the reading nook near the window. A low armchair. A table with tea rings. A shadow.

"She was extraordinary," she said. "Fierce. Quietly furious."

"You knew her?"

"I watched her once," Nora said. "She drew the same church tower every day for a week. Each time from a different angle. But the ivy never changed."

"She's not in any of the artist registries."

"She wouldn't be."

Annabel hesitated. "Did she live here?"

"No. But grief travels. People follow it like a trail."

***

Nora reached under the counter and placed a book down.

Not a title.

A notebook.

Leather-bound. Blank on the outside.

"She left this with someone. Not me."

"Who?"

"She said to wait for someone to ask the right questions."

***

Annabel reached for it.

Nora placed a hand on top.

"You're not the only one asking."

***

Annabel felt a prickle on the back of her neck.

Turned.

There was no one there.

Just the soft rustle of pages.

***

Outside, across the street, a figure in a dark coat moved behind the glass of the tea shop window.

Not facing them.

But watching.

***

Persephone leapt down, brushed against Nora's legs, and growled.

Low.

And long.

Chapter 13

Annabel waited until night to open the notebook.

Not out of fear. Out of respect.

The fire was low. The tea had gone cold. Persephone was curled like a comma beside her, tail twitching softly in her sleep.

Evie sat across from her, arms crossed, watching like she was waiting for a spell to backfire. "Ready to summon your ghost artist?" she asked.

Annabel didn't smile. She opened the cover.

***

There was no name. No date.

But the first page had a drawing.

An archway. Overgrown. Precise and delicate.

Underneath, one sentence in a looping hand:

"Truth is rarely about what happened. It's about who remembers it."

***

They turned page after page. Sketches. Notes.

Bits of poems.

Colour tests.

All of it... *Isolde's.*

But near the back, the pages changed.

The handwriting shifted.

The tone grew *colder.*

"She tried to give her a way out."

"Elena said she'd 'earned' it."

"She didn't understand that talent isn't a thing you take. It's a thing that breaks when you touch it."

***

Evie whispered, "These aren't Isolde's anymore."

Annabel nodded.

"This is someone *writing about her.* After the fact."

"Who?"

"No idea."

They reached the final page.

Nothing but a quote, scrawled with force:

"I loved her once. But I loved what she believed in more."

***

The knock came just after midnight.

Three soft raps.

Not hurried. Not polite.

Just... deliberate.

Annabel and Evie exchanged a look.

Persephone stood up; tail fluffed like a feather duster full of secrets.

***

At the door: a small brown envelope.

No stamp. No address.

Just one word: "*Stop.*"

***

Ravi was already waving when they walked in the post office the next morning.

"Don't ask why I'm still caffeinated, I don't even know," he said. "OH, also —
weird thing. You ready?"

Evie leaned on the counter. "Always."

Ravi pulled out a parcel record book, flipped a few pages, and tapped one line.

"A pigment tin was delivered here two weeks before the retreat. No return address. No name. Just initials: '*I. V.*'"

Annabel felt her stomach drop.

Ravi added, "I wasn't supposed to log it. Elena asked me to... you know... forget it existed."

"Did you see who left it?"

"No. But—"

He paused. Frowned. Checked another line.

"Wait. That's weird."

"What?"

"There's *another parcel.* Last week. Same handwriting. Different recipient."

"Who?"

Ravi turned the book toward them.

A single name. Written in the same looping, unfamiliar hand.

Claudia Voss.

Chapter 14

The studio door was open.

Just slightly.

Enough for the morning air to drift in.

Enough for Annabel to stop mid-step and feel her whole-body freeze.

"I locked that," she whispered.

Evie, behind her, didn't speak.

Just stepped forward slowly.

Persephone slipped in ahead of them like a shadow with a mission.

***

Inside, the space looked untouched — *at first.*

The same pale light.

The same quiet.

The same chill.

But then, the coat that had been on the chair was gone.

The final canvas — the unfinished one of Witch's Hollow — had been turned around.

And the *drawer Annabel had found the sketchbooks in... was empty.*

***

Evie crouched beside it.

"Gone. All of them."

Annabel stood still, scanning the room.

The pigment tin.

The brooch.

The envelope.

All *still at the cottage.*

This wasn't about removing the evidence.

This was about *removing the motive.*

***

A single sheet of paper was left in the drawer.

Folded.

Evie opened it carefully.

One word. Inked dark. Sharp. Almost angry.

"*Enough*".

***

Persephone was already near the windowsill.

She pawed once at the ledge.

Annabel followed her gaze.

Outside: a *footprint.*

Faint. Shallow.

Someone had stood there.

Watched.

Then walked away.

***

Evie exhaled, slow and furious.

"They're cleaning up."

Annabel nodded. "And getting bolder."

"They took the sketchbooks."

"Because they're afraid of what's inside."

"No," Evie said softly.

"They're afraid *you'll put it all together.*"

***

Annabel's hand hovered over the drawer. Empty now. Too quiet.

"They want the story to stay incomplete," she murmured.

***

She stood suddenly.

Evie blinked. "Where are you going?"

Annabel was already grabbing her coat.

"To find someone who might know what it was supposed to say."

Chapter 15

Beatrice was alone in the tearoom, sleeves rolled up, wiping down counters even though they were already clean.

There was a tray of lemon biscuits untouched on the table.

She looked up when Annabel entered.

Paused.

Then sighed.

"I was wondering when you'd come."

***

They sat by the window.

Outside, the sky was that soft gold-grey that comes before a storm.

Inside, the silence was heavier than the air.

***

Beatrice didn't speak at first. Just poured tea.

She didn't ask if Annabel wanted any.

She just *knew*.

Then she said:

"I knew Elena wasn't well. Before this all started."

Annabel blinked. "How?"

Beatrice hesitated, then spoke slowly.

"We'd crossed paths at retreats before," she said softly. "Always professionally. But there was a moment once — after a particularly harsh critique — when she asked me to sit with her. Just for a moment. Said I had a calming face."

"She came to me again a few months ago. Asked if I'd ever... heard of someone named Isolde Voss."

***

Annabel froze.

Beatrice went on, voice quiet.

"I said no. Not at first. But the name felt familiar. Like something I'd overheard once — a conversation at a gallery, years ago."

"Elena looked... shaken. She said someone was contacting her. Sending old sketches. Reminding her of work she hadn't touched in decades."

"She asked me if she should be afraid."

Annabel leaned forward. "And what did you tell her?"

Beatrice looked down at her tea.

"I told her yes."

***

There was a long pause. The kind that feels like it's holding more than silence.

Then Annabel asked, "Why didn't you say anything before?"

Beatrice finally met her eyes.

"Because I wasn't sure who the message was meant for.

Elena... or someone else still listening."

***

She hesitated again. Then added:

"Elena was fraying at the edges long before she came here.

She tried to lead the room. But she always kept one hand clenched in her pocket.

Like she was afraid something would fall out."

"And when she asked me about Isolde...

It wasn't just fear.

It was *recognition*."

Chapter 16

The cottage was quiet except for the wind whispering past the windows.

Annabel sat at the table, hands resting on a folded piece of paper.

Not new.

Not unfamiliar.

Just finally, *ready to be read properly.*

Elena's note.

I found the truth. But not where I thought it was.

The first time she'd read it; Annabel had felt confusion. The words had seemed cryptic, half-spoken, like something scribbled mid-thought. But now, after everything—after the sketchbooks, after the pigment tin, after Beatrice's confession—it felt different.

Not like a warning.

More like a goodbye.

Or a confession.

Beatrice's voice echoed in her mind:

She wasn't worried about being caught.

She was worried someone remembered.

Annabel unfolded the paper again and laid it on the table, next to the other fragments she'd gathered. The label from the parcel Ravi had let her photograph. A printed scan of one of the sketchbook pages. And the short, sharp note they'd found in the empty drawer at the studio.

Only one word in black ink and in bold.

Enough.

She leaned forward, letting her eyes drift over each. They were all handwritten. All different in tone. But they didn't feel like four separate voices. Just... two.

The parcel label and the handwriting in the second half of the sketchbook had the same deliberate slant. The same pressure in the strokes, the same habit of tightening the loop on a lowercase "e." Whoever had written them had a steady hand and something to prove. There was emotion there, but it was buried under control.

The "Enough" note, though—it was from the same person, but it wasn't the same writing. Not exactly. The pressure was harder. The slant slightly sharper. Like whoever wrote it had been holding their breath the entire time. It was colder. Final. As if they'd decided, at the last moment, that something needed to end.

And then there was Elena's.

Loose. Looped. Emotionally open in a way the others weren't. She had written that line without thinking too hard about it, and that was what made it so striking now. It was the only one that didn't feel like part of a plan. It felt like the truth.

Persephone jumped onto the table and, with the slow precision of someone who believed she owned every surface in the house, sat squarely on the "Enough" note. She stared at Annabel like this had been her idea all along.

Annabel didn't move her.

Her eyes drifted again to the sketchbook scan. The boldness of the strokes. The calm fury. It wasn't Claudia's hand. And it certainly wasn't Elena's. Not Basil. Not Beatrice.

So, who?

Who would care enough to send pigment tins to Elena and Claudia?

Who would bury a brooch with the same ivy-covered chapel sketched in enamel?

Who would erase the sketchbooks from the studio, yet leave a note behind?

And—most importantly—who would carry someone else's pain so fiercely they'd spend years keeping a ghost alive?

She whispered it aloud without meaning to.

"It wasn't about revenge.

It was about memory."

The wind outside shifted. A low branch scratched against the side of the house, slow and soft like fingers brushing glass.

Annabel picked up Elena's note again and read the line one last time.

Not where I thought it was.

Maybe the truth hadn't been a revelation.

Maybe it had been a surrender.

She folded the paper slowly and looked at Persephone, who gave her a single tail flick of approval.

"I need to talk to Claudia," she said quietly.

Persephone blinked once.

And didn't move from the note.

Chapter 17

Claudia didn't answer the door right away.

Annabel stood in the cool morning mist, coat pulled tight, Persephone pacing silently at her feet like she knew the stakes had changed. A breeze stirred the ivy crawling up the fencepost. The air smelled like wet stone and fading lavender.

Then the door opened.

Claudia stood barefoot in a paint-smudged jumper; hair twisted up in a loose knot. Her eyes were red, but not fresh-red — the kind worn from too many nights pretending sleep was coming.

"You're not here to accuse me, are you?" she asked.

Annabel shook her head. "No. I'm here because I don't think this is just about you."

***

They sat by the window in Claudia's sitting room, mugs of tea growing cold between them. Persephone claimed the rug beneath the radiator like she was part of the upholstery.

Annabel placed Elena's note on the table between them.

Claudia didn't touch it.

"She wrote that before she vanished," Annabel said. "But I don't think it was fear. I think it was surrender."

Claudia let out a bitter breath. "She knew she didn't deserve what she had."

Annabel looked at her carefully. "You said you came here to watch her unravel."

"And I did."

"But someone else helped her fall."

***

Claudia went still.

Her voice, when it came, was barely audible.

"Sometimes I thought... I saw my mother."

Annabel didn't move.

"In a crowd. A mirror. Once at an exhibition in Berlin—I could've sworn I saw her standing by the entrance. Same coat. Same posture. She didn't even look at me. And by the time I turned around, she was gone."

She laughed once, softly. Not happy.

"I thought I was imagining it. That I was trying to see her. My brain just... wanting her back."

***

Later that afternoon, Claudia found herself in the tearoom, without really deciding to go.

Beatrice was wiping down tables with quiet efficiency, humming something tuneless and low.

Claudia stood in the doorway for a moment before saying, "I saw her again."

Beatrice didn't flinch. Didn't frown. She looked up and studied Claudia's face.

Then, in a tone soft as a dropped handkerchief, she said, "You're not the only one who's seen her."

Claudia stared at her. "You mean... you saw someone who looked like—"

Beatrice nodded once. "Near the woods. The chapel path. I thought it was grief playing games. But it wasn't just you."

***

They sat in silence.

Claudia turned her teacup in her hands.

"Why wouldn't she come to me?" she asked. "If someone who looked like her—if it was her—why wouldn't she say something?"

Beatrice's answer was simple, but heavy. "Maybe she didn't think you were ready. Or maybe she didn't know if she could bear to be seen."

Claudia said nothing.

But something in her posture shifted.

A slow tilt from mourning... to wondering.

***

Later, as the sky bruised into evening, Annabel met Evie outside the shop with a notebook in her hand and a new edge to her step.

"She saw her," Annabel said. "Claudia saw someone she thought was her mother."

Evie raised an eyebrow. "Thought?"

"She's not imagining things."

She paused.

"And neither was Beatrice."

***

Somewhere deep in Witch's Hollow, a bird startled from its perch and took flight.

And under the earth, the truth waited.

Not where they thought it was.

But right where it had been laid to rest.

Chapter 18

She had buried her sister's ghost long ago.

But Elena's shadow lingered longer.

In the weeks after the retreat began, Idomene watched from the edge of Witch's Hollow, hidden beneath the hood of a coat that once belonged to someone she loved too much to forget. She traced Elena's movements with her eyes, marked the way her voice cracked mid-sentence, the hesitation in her brushwork, the soft tremor in her hands.

The pigment had begun to work by then.

She hadn't planned it as a death. Not at first.

It was supposed to be a *decline.*

A graceful unravelling.

The kind of fading Elena had *inflicted* on others.

But then Elena wrote the note.

I found the truth. But not where I thought it was.

That was the moment Idomene knew: the end had to be quiet.

Controlled.

Finished.

So, when the final moment came, she was there.

Elena was alone.

The tea was warm.

The brush fell from her hand like a dropped verdict.

And Idomene buried her — not in shame, but in *silence.*

The kind Isolde never got.

***

Claudia didn't know why she was walking toward Witch's Hollow.

The wind was sharp. The sky hung low. But something inside her was... pulled. Not by logic. Not by curiosity. By *grief that no longer fit inside her skin.*

Behind her, footsteps.

She turned.

Persephone.

The cat walked without sound, ears forward, tail level like a question mark half-drawn.

She didn't meow. Didn't break pace.

She just walked beside Claudia.

Like a guide.

Like a witness.

****

The ivy was thick.

Too thick.

Claudia stepped off the path, her boot sinking slightly into moss. Persephone stopped ahead, just before the line of trees thickened.

She sat.

Didn't move.

Didn't follow.

Claudia stepped forward.

The scent hit her first. Faint, but undeniable. Earth and oil. A trace of something metallic.

Then she saw the hand.

Half-buried. Pale. One finger still curled around the *shattered shaft of a paintbrush.*

Claudia let out a sound — a choked, fractured breath — and staggered backward, heart punching her ribs from the inside.

She turned, started to run—

Her foot caught a root.

The fall was fast, brutal. Her shoulder hit the earth first. Then her cheek. Pain bloomed bright and hot across her ribs. She gasped; breath knocked clean from her lungs.

***

Footsteps.

Not hurried.

Measured.

Soft.

Then a voice, gentle and unbearably familiar:

"Don't move. You'll make it worse."

Claudia tried to turn.

A hand touched her forehead — warm, callused, careful.

And then she saw her.

Same face.

Same eyes.

But older. Wiser.

Not a ghost.

Not a hallucination.

A woman.

Alive.

"You're not her," Claudia whispered. "You're not my mother."

"No," the woman said softly. "But I was once her shadow."

"Who are you?"

The woman's mouth trembled. Not with sadness. With *relief.*

"My name is Idomene Voss. Isolde was my twin sister. Our parents loved classical literature rooted in myth and legend. Thus, our names: Isolde from Tristan and Isolde and Idomene from Trojan War and Greek mythology."

***

Persephone stepped forward, brushed against Idomene's leg, and sat quietly beside them.

She looked at Claudia like she already knew.

And perhaps... she did.

Chapter 19

Claudia sat on the edge of the low stone wall, her ankle wrapped and elevated, her hands clenched in her lap.

Idomene knelt nearby, brushing moss from her coat like it mattered.

Neither of them spoke. Persephone lay between them, curled like a sphinx on watch, tail occasionally flicking with quiet judgment.

The trees murmured with wind. Somewhere in the distance, a wood pigeon called. The world was going on — *as if it hadn't shifted forever.*

Finally, Claudia said, "Why?"

Idomene didn't look at her. "Because your mother did not want to be seen at first. But Elena made sure she never was at all."

"And because I couldn't let that theft be the last word."

***

Claudia swallowed. Her voice cracked.

"So, you poisoned her?"

Idomene didn't flinch.

"I gave her the same silence she gave Isolde.

She was already disappearing. I... just didn't stop it."

Claudia looked away, jaw trembling.

"You should have come to me."

Now Idomene looked up. Her eyes were shining but dry.

"I thought I'd already failed you once."

***

Annabel stood at the table at her cottage, the pigment tin opened again.

The contents were faintly metallic, with an oily sheen.

Basil sat opposite her; a catalogue spread open between them. A gallery show from twenty years ago.

"That," he said, tapping one photo, "wasn't her."

Annabel leaned closer.

In the glass reflection of a painting — just barely — a second woman.

Same hair. Different coat.

"That was the real artist."

He didn't gloat. Didn't smile.

He just said, "Elena wasn't a fraud in technique.

She was a fraud in story."

***

Persephone jumped onto the table and sat squarely on the catalogue.

Annabel stared down at her.

"She knew," Annabel muttered. "She always knew."

Basil snorted. "She's a cat. They're all conspiracy theorists."

***

The room was dark.

Jules stood with a broken brush in one hand and a glass of wine untouched on the windowsill.

The catalogue lay on the floor. Open.

Page creased.

Photo glaring.

The face he had adored — the genius he had defended — wasn't hers.

Not truly.

"You weren't the genius," he whispered. "You were just the thief."

He let the brush fall. It hit the floor with a quiet thud.

And then he turned to the wall, grabbed the canvas he'd been trying to finish for weeks—

And slashed through it with a palette knife.

***

Claudia stood at the Hollow.

Her face was pale. Her body trembling.

But her voice was clear.

"You're coming with me."

Idomene didn't ask where.

She simply nodded.

Persephone stood, stretched, and led the way — like she'd known the path long before any of them had taken it.

Chapter 20

The chapel ruins were quiet.

Someone had set up folding chairs. No one said who.

A canvas stood on an easel, facing the crowd.

It wasn't Elena's work.

It was one of the sketchbook pieces. The real ones.

Signed in the bottom corner: *I. Voss.*

Not the famous Halberd.

Not the stolen name.

But the one that belonged.

***

Beatrice had brought lemon cake, because some things couldn't be helped.

Basil stood near the back, arms crossed, jaw tight. He hadn't spoken much all morning.

Annabel sat beside Claudia, who looked composed — but hollow.

Like she'd stepped into her mother's skin for the day.

And Idomene?

She stood off to the side, not quite in shadow.

She didn't wear black. She wore *grey.*

Like fog. Like pencil. Like the in-between where all art begins.

***

The crowd wasn't large. But it *was enough.*

Nora from the bookshop. Ravi from the post office.

The pub owner. The fair judge.

Villagers. Painters. People who had whispered.

Now, they listened.

*****

Claudia stepped forward, voice clear and quiet.

"You've seen work like this before.

But you didn't know who made it."

She held up a piece of paper — an early article about Elena's rise.

"This legacy doesn't belong to the name you know.

It never did."

A beat of silence.

Persephone leapt onto the table beside the easel.

Sat.

Approved.

Claudia went on.

"This work was done by my mother. Isolde Voss.

And protected — in silence, in grief — by my aunt, Idomene."

Gasps fluttered. Then stillness.

Idomene stepped forward.

She said nothing.

But she nodded.

And then she knelt and opened a box.

Inside: the original sketchbooks.

She placed them on the table beside the painting.

"For the archive," she said softly. "For memory."

***

No one clapped.

This wasn't applause.

It was *restoration.*

And it was enough.

***

After, people drifted.

Nora left a single wildflower at the base of the easel.

Ravi hugged Claudia without asking.

Beatrice handed Idomene a warm slice of cake and said only, "You held it longer than most could have."

And Jules?

Jules didn't come.

But someone found a single word pinned to the chapel door, written in paint.

"Truth."

No name.

***

That night, Persephone curled in Claudia's lap as she flipped through her mother's sketches.

She paused on one — the chapel, wrapped in ivy.

And in the distance?

Two girls. Twin shadows, hand in hand.

Epilogue

The moon hung low and full, wrapped in wisps of cloud like an old shawl.

Annabel sat on the porch, wrapped in a thick cardigan, sipping tea that had long gone cold. Persephone lounged across her lap, one paw twitching as if she were chasing ghosts in her sleep.

Evie emerged from the kitchen with a tray of toast and jam and absolutely no sense of quiet.

"You do realise we've been murder-adjacent three times in less than a year," she said, dropping into the chair beside her. "I think we're cursed. Or blessed. Possibly both."

Annabel smiled faintly. "You say that like you're not already hoping for the next one."

"Hoping? I've started sharpening pencils and stocking up on biscuits."

They sat in companionable silence for a moment.

The air smelled like wet leaves, smoke, and *the pause before winter.*

Inside, the cottage was warm. Safe.

Outside, the village slumbered.

For now.

***

And then, in the distance — the faint sound of bells.

Not sinister. Not yet.

Just the jingle of sleigh bells and a child's laugh, carried on the wind.

Evie raised an eyebrow.

"Tell me you didn't hear that."

Annabel just sipped her tea.

Persephone's tail flicked once.

Coming Soon in the Little Firling Mysteries...

Murder during the Mistletoe Procession

A Little Firling Mystery – Book Five

As the village of Little Firling prepares for its beloved Mistletoe Procession—a quaint, candlelit tradition said to bring good fortune and rekindle lost love—Annabel, Evie, and Persephone find themselves in the middle of another mystery... this time with frosty footprints, tangled holiday secrets, and one body far too cold to explain.

What begins as a charming rehearsal turns deadly when the "Spirit of the

Season" is found collapsed in the chapel, a mistletoe crown still frozen in her hand.

As festive cheer turns brittle and long-buried grudges crack beneath the surface, a vanished recipe box, stolen traditions, and a letter that was never meant to be found begin to unravel the truth.

Now, as snow blankets secrets and sleigh bells jingle just a little too eerily, the Firling trio must unwrap a case where *even the most peaceful carol has a darker verse.*